This book

belongs to

....

....

....

For all our babies!
Jaye, Merlin, Finn, Sorley,
Loki and Poppy

First published in Great Britain in 1998 by Levinson Books Ltd.
Published in this edition in 2001 by

GULLANE
CHILDREN'S BOOKS

Winchester House, 259-269 Old Marylebone Road,
London, NW1 5XJ

10 9 8 7 6 5 4

Text © Tony Bonning 1998
Illustrations © Sally Hobson 1998

A CIP catalogue record for this title is available from the British Library.

The right of Tony Bonning and Sally Hobson to be identified
as the author and illustrator of this work has been asserted by them
in accordance with the Copyright Designs and Patents Act 1988.

hardback ISBN 1 86233 094 8
paperback ISBN 1 86233 145 6

Printed in Belgium

Another Fine Mess

Written by
Tony Bonning

Illustrated by
Sally Hobson

GULLANE
CHILDREN'S BOOKS

There was a knock at Fox's door,
    "Post!" called a squeaky voice.

Fox had been out all night and his eyes
were still half closed. He opened the door
and a letter was thrust under his nose.

    "Thanks," he said sleepily and
trudged back to bed.

Fox switched on the lamp and snuggled down
under the duvet to read the letter.

'Dear Nephew,' it said,
'I will pay you a visit
at the next full moon.
Sincerely, Uncle Ferdinand.'

Fox looked blearily at his calendar.
He saw to his horror that the next
full moon was tonight!

"Oh no!" he wailed.
"The den is a mess!"

Fox took out his broom and swept all round the house until he had a pile of rubbish at the front door.

"Where shall I put it now?" he wondered.

As Fox swept the rubbish along the path that ran round the hill, he noticed a hole in the ground.

"This will do just fine," he said, brushing the rubbish down the hole.

Then he went back to his den to wait for Uncle Ferdinand.

Badger woke suddenly.

Her sett was filled with the most terrible CRASH! as if the roof had fallen in.

She jumped out of bed and there, in the middle of the living room, was a pile of rubbish!

Badger was furious.

"How did that mess get here?"

Badger fetched a broom and swept the rubbish
out of her home, through the wood and into
a deep hole.

"In you go," she said,
as the rubbish tumbled out of sight.

The Rabbit family were just about to have their
salad lunch when the rubbish fell SPLAT!
right on to the middle of the kitchen table.

They were horrified.

"Yuk! What a mess!" shouted the children.
"My lovely lettuce!" cried Mummy Rabbit.
"Grab a brush, everyone!" said Daddy Rabbit.

Together the family brushed the rubbish off the table,
out of their burrow and round the hill.

They found a thick clump of grass in which to
hide it, and then they all went home to
make another meal.

Partridge finished pecking around in the wood
and returned to the new nest she had built before lunch.

Partridge was terribly upset to find that someone
had dumped all their rubbish in her nest.

"How could they?" she screeched.
"Some people are just so messy!"

Partridge gathered up some twigs to sweep the rubbish away from her nest.

Finding a hole close by, she brushed the rubbish down the hole.

This done, she went back to her nest to lay some eggs.

Mole was dashing through his house
when the pile of rubbish fell THUMP!
right on top of his head.

"Oh goodness me! Goodness me!
Whatever's that?" he said,
removing a box from his snout.

A few sniffs told him it
was a useless pile of rubbish.

"Can't have this mess in here," he said,
pushing it along his tunnel under the hill.

When Mole reached his front door, he shoved the
rubbish outside. Then he went indoors
to wash his paws.

Meanwhile, all the rubbish rolled
down the hill and landed with a

CLATTER!
BANG! CRASH!

right at the feet of Uncle Ferdinand
who was on his way to see Fox.

"Look at that!" he said
to himself and gathered up the rubbish.

When he reached Fox's den, he left it outside.

"Look at this rubbish I found on the road!"
said an irritated Uncle Ferdinand to Fox when he
answered the door.

"Oh no!" wailed Fox, horrified to see his old rubbish!

He was about to suggest putting it back down the hole he had found earlier, when the Mouse family passed by.

"Look!" exclaimed Mrs Mouse. "Fancy anyone throwing away such wonderful treasures!"

"Help yourself," said Fox with a sigh of relief, as he led Uncle Ferdinand into his home.

"I wish all my
nephews were as
clean and tidy as you,"
said Uncle Ferdinand,
looking around the den.

"I do my best!" said Fox with a sly grin.

GULLANE™
CHILDREN'S BOOKS

Other Gullane Picture Books
for you to read and enjoy:

Stone Soup
TONY BONNING • SALLY HOBSON
hardback: 1 86233 322 X

Harry and the Bucketful of Dinosaurs
IAN WHYBROW • ADRIAN REYNOLDS
hardback: 1 86233 088 3
paperback: 1 86233 205 3

Lucky Socks
CARRIE WESTON • CHARLOTTE MIDDLETON
hardback: 1 86233 258 4

Ordinary Audrey
PETER HARRIS • DAVID RUNERT
hardback: 1 86233 203 7

Billy Bean's Dream
SIMONE LIA
hardback: 1 86233 260 6
paperback: 1 86233 335 1